police 4x4

breakdown truck

air ambulance

police car

lifeboat

17-36

rescue helicopter

lifeguard 4x4

Out and about

scooter

taxi

car

bumper car

motor coach

ice cream truck

train

mobility scooter

tram

double-decker bus

steam train

roller coaster

pickup truck

Ferris wheel

van

On the water

hovercraft

yacht

paddleboat

houseboat

submarine

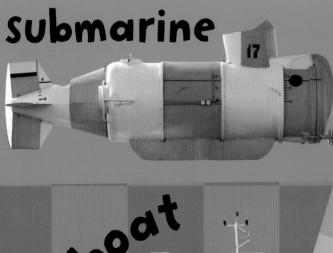

oil tanker

fishing boat

icebreaker

water taxi

cruise ship

seaplane

container ship

hydrofoil

car ferry

barge

Working machines

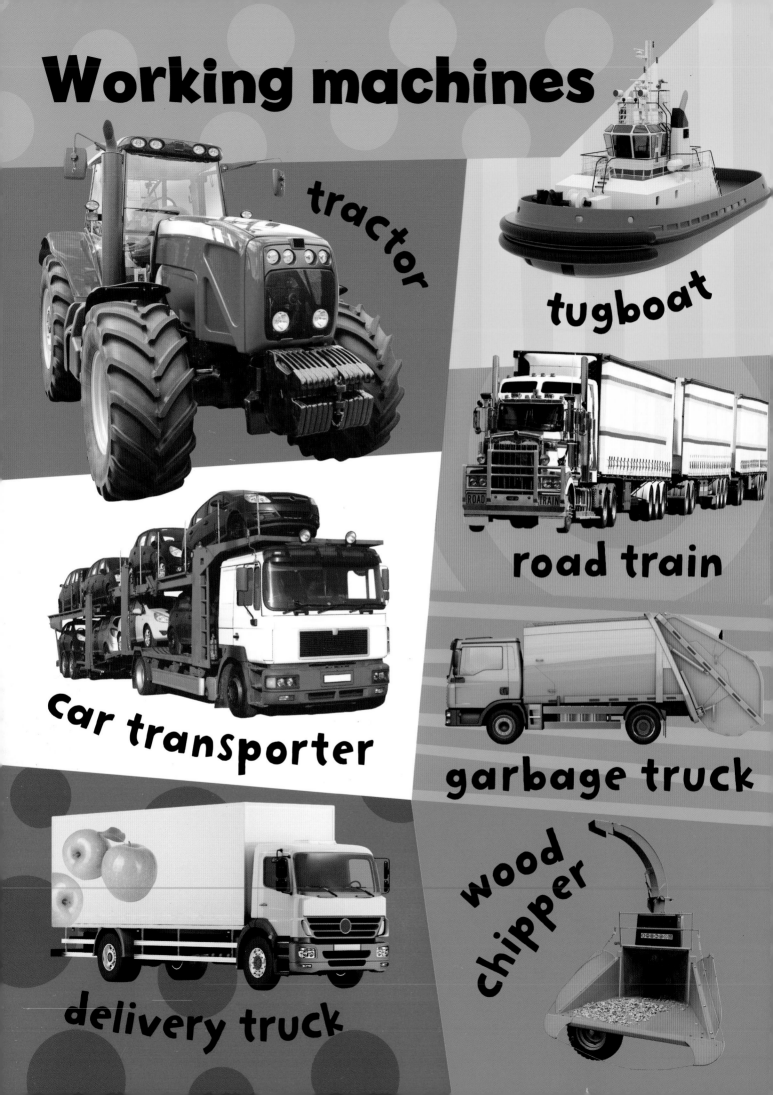

tractor

tugboat

road train

car transporter

garbage truck

delivery truck

wood chipper

forklift

commercial van

tractor-trailer

salt truck

tanker truck

street sweeper

combine harvester

Construction machines

bulldozer

backhoe loader

front loader

cherry picker

grapple skidder

crane

earth drill

scraper

steamroller

cement mixer

dump truck

hooklift truck

flatbed truck

mobile crane

excavator

In the sky

business jet

single-propeller plane

twin-engine airplane

Chinook

firefighting plane

ultralight

airliner

space rocket

airship

military jet

helicopter

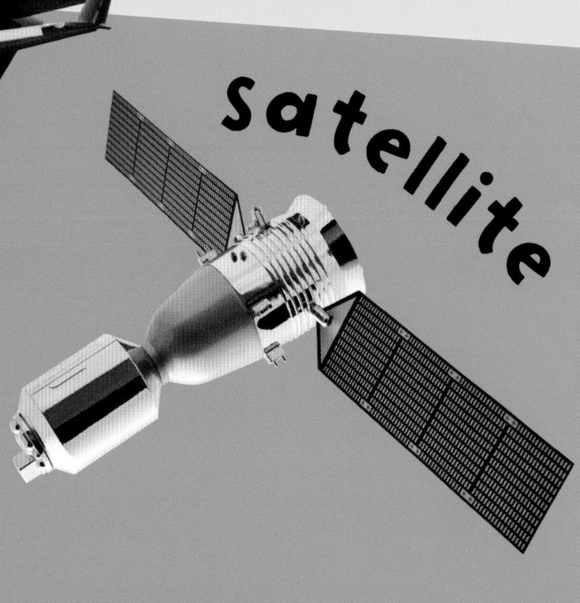

satellite

cargo plane

Sports machines

jet ski

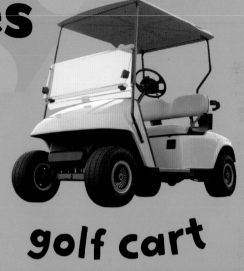
golf cart

Formula One car

ice resurfacer

motocross bike

go-kart

rally car